Martyrs and Holymen

Martyrs and Holymen

LARRY FONDATION

ILLUSTRATIONS BY
KATE RUTH.

Martyrs and Holymen Copyright © 2013
by Larry Fondation

Published by Raw Dog Screaming Press
Bowie, MD

First Edition

Cover & Interior Illustrations: Kate Ruth
Book Design: Jennifer Barnes

Printed in the United States of America

ISBN: 978-1-935738-45-9

Library of Congress Control Number: 2013935257

www.RawDogScreaming.com

Dedication

For Jessica Lee Garrison

Also by Larry Fondation

Acknowledgements

This is a work of fiction. No verisimilitude whatsoever is intended.

Grateful acknowledgment is made to the following publications in which some of these stories appeared, often in somewhat different form:

"Cut Lip" in *Night Train*; "Closed Door Policy," "An Insurrection," and "At Play" in *Prism*; "High Forehead" in *Cal Arts Project* by Kate Johnston; "High Winds" and "Death at Night" in *Brooklyn Rail*; "Swordplay" and "Dirty Girl" at Bringbackpubes.com by Kate Ruth; "Boredom" in *Penny Ante*; "Heroin Chick" in *Smokelong Quarterly*; "Repatriation," "The Common Inquisitor," "Peacekeeper," and "Drones" in *Fiction International*; "Detainees," "Green Eyes," and "Just Outside the Green Zone" in *Flaunt*; "Confrontation," "Hong Kong Hotel," and "Pregnant Girl" in *Dark Sky*; "Little Joy" in *The Industrial Worker Book Review*; "Kandahar" in *Compressed Fiction*; "Dirty Girl" in *Slake*; "A Fucking Band-Aid," "Lynddie," and "Roadside" in *Iconograph*; "Pedicure" and "Platinum Girl" appeared in the anthology, *Oulipo Pornobongo: Anthology of Erotic Wordplay* and "Darkness Drops" and "Don't Ask, Don't Tell" in the anthology *Send My Love and a Molotov Cocktail!: Stories of Crime, Love and Rebellion*, edited by Gary Phillips and Andrea Gibbons (PM Press: Oakland, CA. 2011).

TABLE OF CONTENTS.

Introductory Rites

Creeps

Interlude

Heroes

Closing Rites

Epilogue

Introductory Rites

Dominus vobiscum

I leaned in to kiss her
and she kissed back. I
could taste her blood.

Cut Lip

She had a cut lip. That's what attracted me; that's why I approached her. The cut lip and her eyeshadow.

She was sitting at the bar. I thought she'd be tough, that she'd brush me off. At first I just stood there. I didn't say a thing.

The bar was called The Stardust. It was dimly lit, but not completely dark. I could see her wound clearly. Perhaps it was still bleeding a little. I couldn't be sure. In any case, there was blood on her chin as well—dried or fresh I couldn't say.

Someone had put a lot of money in the jukebox. They were playing bad songs.

I don't suppose it mattered, though at the time I thought it would.

She spoke first.

"Do you want to know what happened to me?" she asked.

"No," I said.

The bartender brought her drinks regularly and without asking.

A fight broke out behind us. Neither of us turned around to look.

I stroked the back of her left hand. I wasn't sure how she would react. We hadn't exchanged another word.

My old girlfriend used to call me "babycakes." I was sure this girl wouldn't call me anything.

I leaned in to kiss her and she kissed back. I could taste her blood.

I led her out of The Stardust by the hand, and she came with me.

Outside there were no shadows. I think our shadows died. There was nothing else either. No other buildings, no cars, no other people. The landscape was full of nothing at all. We walked away, down the dark street, holding onto each other, towards the end of night.

Elles (Woman in a Corset)

We walked up a short flight of stairs to the room.

We had been drinking all night in a doorway. We sipped whiskey—elegantly—from a brown paper bag.

Everything was pale—the room, her skin, the light.

There was no brown, only beige; no red, only pink; no black, only gray.

She kept her shirt on while we made love.

Afterwards, I rolled her shirt up from her waist to see her breasts. The shirt remained around her shoulders.

I left long before dawn, or maybe she did, I don't remember. Perhaps I woke up in her apartment; perhaps she woke up in mine. I don't know.

I was alone.

I felt so good.

**

When we look at a star, we see things that happened a million years ago, or much more.

So it is with our lives. We only understand what has happened to us—our events, their effects—long afterwards, much later.

**

We are walking somewhere, down a street, to a café; we are standing on the corner, playing at the park—it doesn't matter; it is always the same: three of us, all together, three altogether, our triad, our trinity. She is always there and so am I, and a small child who is ours....

Creeps

Oremus!

Closed Door Policy

We pulled at the door of the bar.

"It's not open," I said.

"Kick the door in," she said.

It had been a nice enough evening so far—a decent first date in Hollywood bars. Musso and Frank. The Frolic Room. Now this place she picked was closed.

"I want a drink," she said.

"We can go someplace else."

"I want to drink here."

So I kicked in the door.

I held my breath, but there was no alarm.

There was a flashlight and a pair of gloves placed on a stool by the door, probably the janitor's, and a time clock with a rack of employee punch cards nearby on the wall. I couldn't find the light switch right away so I used the flashlight. Angie sauntered right up to the bar.

I had second thoughts about turning on the lights when she called out:

"Turn on the lights and make me a drink."

"Someone might see us," I said.

"I can't see shit."

I rummaged around behind the bar and found stacks of votive candles and I spread them out on the bar and I lit them with matches that I had in my pocket.

"The cops will just think the staff is working late, cleaning up or something," she said.

"What'll you have?" I asked her. I was starting to get into it.

"Jack and Coke."

We partied hard. I poured call drinks and well drinks and we made out and got drunk and I smashed bottles and glasses against the wall, and so did she.

In the middle of one deep kiss, a huge cockroach crawled across the candlelit bar.

When she saw the giant bug, she screamed, she freaked out, and she ran immediately for the door. I followed her, exiting quickly, leaving the drinks half-drunk and the candles still burning on the brass bar top.

I followed her to her car, her screams rising in odd fear and anger, and without thinking I jumped into the driver's seat. Her keys were half hanging out of the front pocket of her jeans.

Forest fires were raging to the north and south and east, and the 3 AM sky seemed red and hazy.

I tried to put my arm around her to comfort her as we drove east on Santa Monica Boulevard, but the moment was lost and she would have none of it.

She stopped screaming, she started sobbing, then she passed out. I kept staring at her sleeping, heaving body, the crying still causing an occasional hiccupping of her chest as she breathed.

I saw the stuff on the street, tatters and blankets, but the blankets seemed empty, discarded into the right lane of the road.

As soon as I struck the pile, I knew I'd hit more than a bundle of rags. I'd hit skunks before, even a dog once.

I was going 40 miles an hour, maybe more.

The tires and shock absorbers reacted to the body and I swore I could hear the sound of breaking bones.

I guessed that a drunk had rolled off the bus bench where he was sleeping and out onto the street.

She slept soundly in the passenger seat. She didn't stir.

I didn't stop.

I kept driving east towards downtown; I thought I recalled that she had a hotel room there, but I couldn't remember the specifics—just moving back to LA from the Bay Area, something like that.

I got on the 101 off Santa Monica near Western and then I went south on the 110 and got off on Wilshire. The streets were empty.

I pulled up outside the Wilshire Grand Hotel. It didn't seem quite right, but it was as close a memory as I could conjure at the time and given the circumstances.

She was snoring beside me.

I popped the automatic lock, leaned over her and pushed the door open.

The bellman and the valet shot me a look. They couldn't figure out what was going on, didn't know my agenda or what to expect.

I pushed her unconscious ass out the door and onto the pavement. She rolled on the ground a bit, but not like in the movies. I still don't think she woke up—not that I waited around to see…I took off as fast as I could without garnering any more attention than I already had.

The hotel staff rushed to her side.

They would probably abandon her later—maybe call the cops to come get her—when they realized she was not an official guest of the hotel. In that case, I figured she'd sleep it off at the local precinct. If, on the odd chance I was right about her hotel, they'd probably carry her up to her room, shaking their heads, but covering it up as best they could so there wouldn't be a scene.

I really didn't know what would happen to her, and I didn't really care.

Without her, alone in her rental car, I drove back west on Wilshire into the smoky, Southern California night.

Tit for Tat

She was holding her son's hand. Still he got away.

The bus was driving fast.

The boy ran out in front of the bus.

I grabbed his arm, yanked him hard, pulled him out of harm's way.

He didn't even realize what had happened.

His mother did.

"Thank you," she said. "Thank you so much."

"I really need a blow job," I said.

"What?" she said, disbelieving.

"I saved your kid's life," I said. "I want you to suck my dick."

I didn't exactly force her, but I pushed hard for what I wanted.

It was nearly dark.

She took me back to her apartment.

It was a nice place, well put together. She had knick-knacks and a wet bar.

She put her son to bed; I waited patiently for her to do so.

After her boy had gone to sleep, she unzipped me. I was already stiff. She sucked me long and hard and good. I came strong in her mouth and she swallowed. I said thank you and goodbye and I left her place. I walked the two miles home.

High Forehead

For once, I am drinking at a nice place.

The chick across the bar from me has a high forehead. She looks like Elizabeth I.

I want to marry her—or at least run away with her.

**

Most of my friendships are with homeless people. My relationships are short-lived. Not by choice. It's just that these people move around too much. They're outside my bank for, like three weeks, then they're gone.

**

Bartending is hard work. Intellectually, I mean. Jill does this thing. She's so fast. She takes orders, and she pours, and she takes money, and she does it all at once. But she won't date me. I mean I've never asked, but I just know.

**

Downtown, on Skid Row, the girls will go out with me. I like that.

**

I get so embarrassed when I talk to women. I get tongue-tied. Not when I'm downtown. Not on Skid Row. Not at the King Eddie Saloon. I'm kind of a player there.

**

Elizabeth the First is beautiful.

Atypically, I am supremely confident with her.

I ask her out.

She says yes.

On our first date, I ask her to marry me—or run away with me.

Elizabeth—or whatever her name is—is truly beautiful.

She does not agree to marry me—or to leave with me to anywhere at all.

She looks at me funny.

I think I messed up.

High Winds

The beauty of starkness is the beauty of the harsh and the unforgiving. It is the aesthetic of emptiness and loneliness, belied by the hidden rattle and hum.

I am a child of the city. I largely dislike nature, or at least spending time there.

My exception is the desert. I like my beauty to contain the possibility of meanness.

The opposite of stark is lush. The opposite of lush is stark.

I prefer starkness.

**

The parallels between the desert and the inner city seem to me to be both self-evident and uncanny:

Both stark, the shapes all-vertical and horizontal—with little in between, straight lines, high walls—covered with graphics: graffiti and petroglyphs.

The feeling of abandonment in both places is misleading—these environments are populated in their nooks and crannies, in vacant basements or underground burrows—punctuated by violence: the firing of weapons, the nighttime hunt of the owl, the click of a switchblade, the snake's teeth snapping off the tail of the lizard—frightened, scampering, escaping with a third of its body gone and missing. Surviving still.

Much hidden life. Much nocturnal life. A quality of darkness that is truly dark. Light—when it appears—gloating with glare and a grimace: the halogen streetlight and the desert sun.

Unforgiving.

In harsh locales, the furtive are the best adapted.

Beautiful.

**

I have been to Palmdale and I will go back. Palmdale is both a desert and a slum. Coyotes hunt errant housecats at night, and the homicide rate climbs steeply—in the absence of hills, the dead bodies lie flatter on the pavement.

**

I am prepared to flee. Hot sands beckon.

Sagebrush and succulents. Rounded bushes scattered like clumps of hair. High winds; it hasn't rained in months. The tumbleweeds are balls of fire waiting to happen.

Dirt roads in Los Angeles County. Now and still. An hour's drive outside the nation's second largest city. Avenue P. Avenue R. Avenue T-4. Avenue T-10. Like they have run out of names. Flat barren stretches. Dirt dividing dirt. Waiting again: waiting for rain, waiting for subdivisions. Short days and long nights.

It was 17 degrees this morning in Los Angeles. High desert. The Mojave—28 miles from Edwards Air Force Base, the some-time landing strip of the Space Shuttle. Creosote in clusters. Trucks full of peaches pass me on

Pearblossom Highway. The small, dry, tan-colored hills undulate off the road-side—naked bodies reclining, languishing on the landscape.

With little purpose, I have been here in the Mojave for days now, perhaps weeks. But, just as I wanted, things are blending together now, blurring.

Her nails are painted black. The sun is scarlet. When it drops, there will be no light. At midnight, the sand is black but it glitters. I drink coffee at Carol's Coffee Shop. The bar next door is called The Trap. Soon I will go there to drink. I will order straight whiskey. Nothing fancy. Bourbon. Probably Wild Turkey. When I do, the girl on the next bar stool will be weathered, but beautiful. Her nails will be painted black.

I am trying to limit my world. I think I am succeeding.

The motel is small, about a dozen rooms. I am the only occupant. She comes with me. There is nothing around the place for miles. The radio said the winds would gust tonight, up to 60 miles an hour. Sand whips against the tin-covered door. The room is furnished sparely, sparsely—a bed, a dresser, a chair. The television is bolted to the wall. We have brought in a bottle of liquor in a brown paper bag. We have already been drinking for hours. Now we drink straight from the bottle, and then from the plastic cups we find in the bathroom. A touch of class. She rubs the back of my hands with her fingertips. Her nail polish is chipped. When she takes off her shirt, her breasts are firm and round. She takes off her boots and her jeans. She lays down, clothesless, on the cheap mattress. She looks every bit like the rolling hills punctuating the landscape just outside our doorstep.

Chicks with Dirty Feet

Her feet are always dirty. I love that. Then she leaves me.

I find another chick with dirty feet. I love to lick her feet clean. When I do, she gets them dirty again really fast. She walks barefoot most of the time.

I'm so happy now, I can't stand it.

It can't last. It doesn't.

I comb the Promenade in Santa Monica and I search Skid Row. I can't connect.

I find a girl who showers every day. Her feet are never dirty. I am full of thwarted longing.

I turn off the hot water heater. Then I shut off the water altogether. I blame the Department of Water and Power. Nothing changes. Nothing ever does. We are still together. I am content, but forlorn. I look around. I always do. To no avail.

Swordplay

A fat lady was practicing swordplay at the park. I had stopped to smoke a cigarette. I don't smoke at home or in my car.

A fat man joined her. They looked like drum majors, or strange samurai. I watched them until I finished smoking. Then I left.

Later on I was in Chinatown, smoking and drinking at a bar in Mei Ling Way. After six or seven drinks, I went for a massage. It was only ten o'clock. For fifty dollars, a skinny Thai chick jerked me off. Because of the alcohol, it took me awhile, but I came good.

I went to another bar.

The fat chick was there, but not the guy.

I asked her if she wanted a drink and she said no. I didn't argue.

When she said no, I knew it was no. I was disappointed, dejected even, but I did not argue—even when I saw her fat sword-playing friend walk in the door as I was walking out.

**

I was alone at the Korean bar, disconnected from the taxi dancing and the buying of drinks when she walked in.

She sat down next to me, and, this time, she let me buy her a drink.

"What do you want to talk about?" she asked.

"Deconstruction," I said.

"There's nothing outside the text," she said.

The bar lights were red and orange.

She took her top off. She was not wearing a bra. Her tits were huge. I kissed both her nipples. She stroked my hair.

I thought other people were staring at us, but they weren't.

Last call came quickly.

I thought her undressing meant something. She thought it meant something else.

When I came back from the men's room, she was gone.

She weighed two hundred pounds, maybe more. Her swordplay had been incredible. It was forever in my brain.

One of the Korean girls came by. I bought a fifth of Glenfiddich and she stayed. The waitress brought water to go with the whiskey.

The lights were still orange and red.

**

I drove by the park everyday. I stopped there. I smoked two or three cigarettes, so I could stay there longer. I never saw the fat girl or the fat guy again.

Pedicure

My brother has a gun. He waves it around. He locks himself in the bathroom.

I am busy painting my mother's toenails.

Brandon screams and swears at the top of his lungs.

"You going to do rhinestones, sweetie?" my mother asks.

"Definitely," I say. "I have a little nail kit I bought."

"Oooh, I'm excited!"

"My family, my ass," Brandon shouts from the bathroom. "Fuck you!"

He smashes something.

"Brandon, shut the fuck up!" I yell.

"What's wrong with him?" my mother asks.

"I don't know."

Brandon is now breaking things in the bathroom.

My little sister is freaking out.

"Mom, are you going to do something?"

"He always gets like this," I say.

Kerry is 14; Brandon is 15; I am 17.

"Are you ready to do the rhinestones yet?"

My mother is gazing at her freshly painted toenails; she is happy.

"I got to put another coat of red on," I say.

"Well, go ahead and do it."

"The first coat has to dry."

"I'm ready when you are!"

I blow on her toenails to dry them more quickly.

"The two of you!" Kerry shudders and storms out of the room.

More stuff is breaking in the bathroom.

"I have a fucking gun!"

Brandon is really nutting up this time.

I am trying to stay calm, but I have to admit the noise is getting to me.

I miss with the polish.

"You got some on my toe!"

I use a Q-tip to make the pedicure perfect again.

"Mom, give me a sec. I'm going to try and talk to him."

"OK, son. I'll wiggle my toes while you're gone."

"They'll dry good that way. I'll be right back."

I bang on the bathroom door. Of course he won't open it.

"Cut the shit, Brandon!"

"Fuck off, Eric. I'm going to shoot myself!"

"I have no idea what to do with you."

"Eric!!"

My mother is calling for me.

I punch the bathroom door.

"Brandon, you're an asshole!"

Glass breaks.

I return to my mother's toes.

"They're really dry now. Don't they have to be wet and sticky for the rhinestones?"

I kneel at her feet. She has really pretty feet.

It gets louder in the bathroom.

Kerry comes back and sees me on my knees.

"Are you two going to do something?"

I go back to the bathroom.

"Brandon, what the fuck?"

"What the fuck is he doing in there?"

It is my mother's voice.

She stands next to me, salon separators between her toes.

"Brandon Allen Commings, come out of that bathroom right now!"

"Fuck you, Mom!"

The gun goes off.

I kick down the door.

Inside the bathroom, there is a hole in the wall, but Brandon is fine.

"Give me the gun."

He hands me the pistol.

"Go to sleep."

Brandon trots off.

My mother kisses me. I put my arm around her and kiss her too.

Kerry and Brandon stomp and sob for a while, then everything is quiet.

My mother and I return to the couch.

"Will you finish doing my toenails now?"

Dirty Girl

Pieces of dog shit dot the floor of her apartment. Wanda owns a dog but she never takes it for a walk. It shits inside. Sometimes she cleans it up, sometimes she doesn't. It sits there and eventually dries up. But it's not just the dog shit. Her whole place is a mess: piles of dirty dishes, empty beer cans and wine bottles, unwashed clothes strewn about.

She doesn't shower very often either. Every couple of weeks. She smells a little but not much given how infrequently she bathes. She's popular at all the clubs. Men love her. She always has a boyfriend.

Her romances all seem to last about a year. They end with the boy screaming, "You're gross!" I can never figure that out. She's the same the whole time. It's like, after a year, they realize just how unclean she really is. But it always seems to work that way for Wanda. She doesn't seem to care. A week or two later, she's got another guy.

Her circle of friends is once removed from mine, but we hang out at the same places. I first meet her at The Shortstop on Sunset. The bartenders there are good, but there are too few of them, so you have to wait forever for a beer. Wanda is standing next to me. I can smell her a little but I like it. She smells like sex and sweat.

We order the same drink—Irish and soda—and we laugh about it.

"You buying?" she asks. She is teasing but I can't tell at first.

Her hair is greasy but she has a sly smile, sexy for sure.

She tells me she already has a boyfriend but we exchange numbers at the end of the night anyway.

**

The first time I go to her place, I can't believe it. It looks like the set of a movie about degradation and squalor. I come in anyway. She hands me a cold beer.

Evidence of her boyfriend abounds—large-size Chucks and men's underwear on the floor.

"My boyfriend's out of town," she says.

We flirt but do nothing.

We talk a lot about music and bands and drink a lot of beer.

At about three, I head home.

**

I lose my job at Sea Level Records because they close the store.

I start hanging around with Wanda most afternoons.

When we are out, she has to be home by three in the afternoon everyday because she gives her 8th Grade neighbor a blow job when he comes home from school.

The kid is a little Latino guy.

"You want to watch?" she asks me.

"No," I say, but I do not leave.

"My boyfriend won't watch either," she says.

She takes the kid in the bedroom.

Ten minutes later, they are done and the kid goes home.

She looks at me.

"What?" she says.

I don't say anything.

It's usually easy for us to talk, but now I am kind of quiet.

"It helps with his confidence," she says "He used to flunk every subject, now he's getting straight A's."

Sure enough she pulls out a couple of copies of his report cards—a steady rise in his performance, I admit.

"Don't be judgmental," she says. "He's a boy, not a girl."

**

Two days later I watch.

Sergio is glad to have me play the voyeur. He is proud and happy and puffing up his tiny chest.

He smiles widely when Wanda swallows.

I want to tell him that Wanda and I have never touched each other but it is not appropriate.

When they are done, Sergio asks for a beer.

"You're too young to drink," Wanda says and sends him on his way.

"When he hits the 9th grade, goes to high school, I gotta cut him off," she says. "He needs a girlfriend."

"You're right about that," I say.

"You hungry?" she asks me.

She microwaves me some Costco taquitos.

While we are eating her dog takes a dump on the floor.

I offer to take the dog for a walk.

"A little late," she says. She laughs and points at the pile of shit.

She goes to the fridge and grabs two cans of Pabst.

"Besides, you'll spoil him," she says.

**

I begin to drop by unannounced.

Today she is reading. She reads a lot in fact.

"You like Kant?" she asks me.

"The categorical imperative?"

"I prefer 'a'."

"'A'?"

"Yeah, the indefinite article…"

"OK."

"I love The German Idealists."

She is reading a Penguin paperback anthology with that title. She puts her book down and smiles at me.

"Especially Hegel."

Her phone rings.

She has a steel blue iPhone. She keeps the volume up. I can always hear both sides of her conversations.

Now a man shouts from the other end. Clearly it is her boyfriend. He is still out of town. I am not sure where he is. She has not told me. But he is very angry and loud.

He yells for about ten minutes straight.

She says nothing.

I pick up her book and, without losing her page, begin to read the introduction. It sounds interesting.

When her boyfriend finishes his tirade, she turns off her phone.

She looks at me. I can't tell if she is sad.

"I guess I'm single again," she says.

We kiss for the first time.

**

Wanda is always fully clothed when she services Sergio. Not today. She is wearing her bathrobe with nothing on underneath. Her breasts poke through the folds of the robe.

I have only watched their escapades twice. Today she pleads with me to be with them.

She does him right by the front door of her apartment. She works extra quickly. He is staring down at her tits. He comes extra quickly. He waits for her to swallow but this time she does not. She hurries him out the door while he is still zipping up his pants.

"Tomorrow?" he asks.

This is different, and young Sergio is confused.

"Yes," she mumbles with her mouth full.

She shuts and locks the door behind him.

As soon as he is gone she flings her robe to the floor.

She is naked and sweaty.

"Kiss me," she says.

I do.

We tongue and kiss with all the extra wetness and I am hard as mahogany.

We finish kissing.

"Lick me clean and fuck me!"

I unbutton my shirt and drop to my knees. I fumble with my pants as I work my tongue up her thighs. She spreads her legs as she stands, shuffling her feet further apart on the unwashed hardwood floor. My tongue parts her labia.

I am Wanda's boyfriend now.

Up, Up and Away

She doesn't want me, so I kidnap her.

It's really easy.

You don't have to try real hard, or want to real baldly.

Arma virumque cano.

I know what I am talking about.

I pick her up after school.

I have done it so many times.

Back when she wanted to be with me.

So I do it again.

She jumps in my car, eagerly but fearfully.

It used to be always eagerly.

Now there is trepidation.

There's this song by The Fifth Dimension, "Up, Up and Away."

She does not know this song.

I am reading a book called "Warped Passages." It is by a science chick named Lisa Randall. I see her picture on the book jacket. I think she is really cute.

I take this high school chick into the woods. I do not know what to do next.

We have fucked before.

She is not sure whether to be scared or to be excited.

I am both.

I kiss her a couple of times.

She kisses me back.

I think of super-realist painters, like Richard Estes and Chuck Close.

I think of my 6th grade teacher who had really long fingernails. Her name was Ms. Evans. It was right in the middle of the first wave of feminism. So I couldn't determine whether or not she was married. It turned out she was not.

I always liked when she asked me to meet with her, to discuss a paper or some other thing. She was my English teacher.

I tell Lisa to get in the car, and we leave the woods.

She thinks it's a game. I do not.

"This is romantic," she says,

I drive us both back to my apartment.

I drink beer from a can.

I do not speak the whole way.

She talks at first, then not at all.

It is very silent.

Back at my place, I lock Lisa in the closet.

She giggles, then begins to cry.

She starts to cry more.

I can hear her even though the closet door is closed tight.

I turn on the stereo.

I play a variety of music: VU, The Goldberg Variations, Marvin Gaye, Nels Cline, Nas.

Her sounds are muffled.

I clutch my pillows.

After four or five hours, I let her out of the closet.

We kiss, and kiss, and kiss.

I know a pizza place that is still open.

We go there.

The Scholar

I had come from the library. I'd checked out a few books.

It was the start of twilight. Someone yelled "Fuckhead!" as I walked by.

I didn't figure he was talking to me. Then I felt a tug on my LAPL tote bag.

"I'm talking to you, book boy!"

He was wearing a nice track suit.

I hate to get my clothes dirty.

I reached into the pocket of my new Tommy Hilfiger blazer and pulled out my knife and stuck it deep into the man's right shoulder. I stepped out of the way quickly so his blood would not stain my new jacket.

"What the fuck is wrong with you?" the man shouted.

I did not answer.

I cleaned the knife on his sleeve and put it back in my pocket.

I walked to the nearest well-lit bar to have a cocktail and to read my books.

Redondo

He was playing the guitar. A bar on the pier.

She was his girlfriend, I guess. Sitting right up front, by the makeshift stage.

**

Pacific Fish had a long wait. A huge line. The clientele crowding the wharf were speaking Japanese and Spanish, in that order.

I'm sure the place was good, but I had no intention of waiting.

**

The televisions were on mute. There were three: the Yankees vs. the Mets; beach volleyball; the World Cup.

I tried to distance myself, but I failed.

**

A short, fat Mexican kid, maybe four, dropped a red-white-and-blue beach ball over the skinny pier railing. The ball fell down a level, into the sand below. The kid started to cry. My Spanish sucks, but it is not awful. The boy's parents told him the ball was gone; they said he should forget about it, that he ought to move on.

I can never forget a single thing; I never move on.

I vaulted the green rail and retrieved the kid's beach ball.

We exchanged the words "gracias" and "de nada" a half-dozen times.

I returned to the bar with the live music.

**

Through the ample windows, I could see a sharp curve of beach, the coast bending to the south, and scattered clumps of people wading in tepid waves.

I took a seat at the bar.

The music was fine, inviting even—a single musician playing cover songs: Neil Young, Jimmy Buffett, an occasional Bob Marley, the Beatles.

The chick was cute and bored; she'd heard this shit a hundred times, maybe more.

While the guy concentrated on his chord choices, I focused on the girl.

I bought her one drink, then another.

It all happened quickly after that.

We made out while her boyfriend took a break. When he came back to play, we stepped outside for a cigarette.

The sun was almost down and we watched the few remaining beachgoers, splashing and laughing still, or packing up to leave. We made out some more.

Though I wasn't exactly sure where I was going, I asked her to come with me.

She said no. She said it nicely; she said she'd had fun and she said that I was lovely.

She walked back inside to sit near her boyfriend while he played for inattentive beer drinkers. I followed her back inside. I put twenty dollars in the man's tip jar. I told her I had to go. She kissed me once more, but this time it was on the cheek. I waved as I walked out the door.

**

Out on the pier, the crowd hadn't thinned, only changed. It had turned dark. A taqueria had scores of bikers inside and cheap beer on tap. It was an open-air place, so there was no real threshold to distinguish in from out. Nonetheless I hesitated before stepping inside.

Piss Girl

She was in the middle of pissing in my mouth when the doorbell rang.

"Come in," she said. "It's open."

"What the fuck are you thinking?" I asked.

Carla and I were on the living room floor. Joanne walked right in. Carla was still pissing.

"Oh," Joanne said.

She turned to leave.

"I'm almost done," Carla said.

Joanne looked up at the ceiling. She seemed like she might laugh—or not. I'm not sure. She shuffled her feet.

Carla and I were both naked. Carla was squatting over me and she was jerking me off as she peed. As she was finishing up—a strong stream of piss reduced to a dribble—I came in her hand.

As always, it was a great orgasm. I didn't have as much time to be embarrassed as I thought. After my initial panic, in fact, I didn't even think about Joanne at all until after I'd come.

Carla came, too, and when she was done screaming, falling down beside me, we both looked up and Joanne was still standing there. Her expression was different. Carla sensed it, I guess.

"You want a turn?" Carla asked her. "It's fun."

I had thought Joanne was going to split out the door at first sight of all this. I thought she was that kind of girl. I guess I was wrong. I guess I didn't know her so well. Though we all hung out together, she was mostly Carla's friend.

Right away, at Carla's invitation, she kicked off her shoes and slipped off her pants. I stayed on my back, my mouth wide open. Joanne squatted over me. Within seconds, she started to go.

**

Carla and I had begun this piss thing three weeks before Joanne walked in on us. It was her idea.

We were in bed watching TV. We'd just fucked, but in a boring way. We both knew it.

"You know what I've always wanted to do?" Carla asked.

We were eating frozen pizza and watching "House," about a misanthropic, but brilliant, doctor.

I didn't say anything. I wanted her to finish her own thought.

"Piss in a guy's mouth," she said.

"What?"

"It's sensual—the wetness, the sound, the flow, you know…."

"I guess."

"Urine's sterile, you know."

"That's true."

"Besides, it's OK to feel superior sometimes."

I didn't argue the point.

"You think I am weird?"

49

I stroked her hair really nicely.

She cuddled me tight and fell asleep before the show was over.

I turned off the television and the light and I realized I was very hard.

I masturbated while she snored, spooned against my body.

**

A couple of days after Carla proposed her piss idea, I agreed.

I brought it up this time; I knew she wasn't going to mention it a second time. It was my turn.

We'd been together for three years. Sex was still good, but no longer new.

It was a boring Sunday afternoon. I was lounging around in my bathrobe, reading the Sunday New York Times. I hate watching sports, but I was watching a baseball game on TV. It wasn't even an LA team. With nothing else to do, Carla was watching it with me.

I gave her beer after beer.

"You trying to get me drunk?"

I handed her another beer, but I didn't say anything.

After beer number five, she finally got up off the couch.

"Where you going?"

"I gotta pee."

I held her back.

I rolled off the couch—flipping off my bathrobe—and I got down on the floor on my back and I opened my mouth.

I could tell she didn't want to say anything, but she did.

"Are you serious?"

"If you are," I said.

She took her bathrobe off and squatted over me. Her ass, hanging above my face, looked especially nice.

She released in a torrent.

I was hard immediately. She grabbed my cock and stroked it as she pissed. I came before she finished. When she was done, I rolled her over and licked her and sucked her clit in a frenzy, but not so frantic that I couldn't change pace like she likes. Her orgasm was bigger than her piss. We fucked a couple of times before going to bed for a nap, leaving the TV on and blaring.

**

By the time Joanne came over to join in the fun, Carla and I had been pushing the piss play to a high pitch.

We worked a block apart. She'd call at lunch time.

"I gotta go."

We'd find a place to do it. I had a cubicle. No good. She had a private office. That worked. And the bathroom at the nearest Starbuck's had a lock with a key.

After Joanne's visit, we decided to hold a piss party. Only four girls came, but we had quite a night. By the end of it, the girls had drunk nearly two cases of beer; of course, they produced quite a volume of hot clear piss.

They held their fists high in the air:

"Urine-Nation!" they shouted.

**

As with everything under the sun—making money, spending money, staying up all night—piss play got boring.

Our games became less and less frequent, then stopped altogether. We played chess in the nude for a while, but it wasn't the same. We remain wide open—searching even—for the next new thing.

Platinum Girl

Platinum girl starts the whole thing.

My hotel pens fail me, break.

Tijuana is not Juarez, but still they die.

Her nails are bright red.

We are at the Valero Station. Pumping gas, smoking cigarettes.

Los Angeles is a border town.

Inside La Barca we drink.

I have a deal to make but I don't know what it is.

Without a word she rakes my face with her fingernails.

I bleed.

She puts her arm around me and pulls me close.

I kiss both her cheeks.

Guns bark.

The bartender dies.

Patrons drop like flies. Wait: That's so trite. Patrons die of gunshot wounds.

The coroner's list seeps inside my jacket pocket.

We do not move.

I cannot watch the man in the striped shirt die.

Paleontology has its limits.

Bowden, Bolano.

Juana Jimenez, Age 19, Cause of Death –

Graciela Sanchez, Age 14, Cause of Death –

Ana Gomez, Age 22, Cause of Death –

Ad infinitum.

Platinum girl makes me bleed again.

The brink of war.

Of course I encourage her.

She shaves all her hair, all of it.

I love her black dress.

"Please," I say.

"Please what?"

The lights go on and off.

We order another drink.

Drugs and Money

Al and Donna sit on the front steps of their apartment building, waiting for their fifteen year-old son. There are two stairs. They are sitting on the top one; their feet are on the bottom one. Al wears bedroom slippers. Donna's feet are bare. Her toenails are long and dirty. They are dotted with patches of red from polish applied long ago. Behind the couple is a large brown door, partially open, with two panes of perfectly square glass inset about a third of the way down. One of the glass panes is broken. A bare light bulb hangs in the corridor of the building just inside the door. Bugs swarm around the bare bulb. On one wall there are twelve mailboxes, pieces of masking tape scored with faded, hand-lettered names affixed to each one. Six doors open off the hallway. The other six apartments are upstairs.

Al drinks Budweiser from a can. Donna drinks Lite Beer. She wants to keep her weight down.

"He's late," Al says.

"Do you think he's alright?"

"He's alright," Al says.

"Did you watch the game?" Donna asks.

"Piece of shit," Al says. "I turned it off after the fifth inning."

"Did they lose?"

"Shit, twelve to two in the fifth."

"With Valenzuela pitching?"

"No," Al says. "With that guy Oral Roberts or whatever."

"Hershiser," Donna says.

"Yeah. Hershiser or whatever."

Al throws his empty beer can into the gutter. Donna lights a long, brown cigarette.

"You want another beer?" he asks.

"You going inside? Sure, I'll have another one," Donna says.

Some of Donna's fingernails are long; some are short, broken. She starts cleaning them with a matchstick while Al is in the house.

Al comes back with four beers.

"They're gonna get warm," Donna says.

"Drink fast," Al says. "I don't want to get up every five minutes to get beer."

Donna flicks her cigarette butt out onto the sidewalk.

"When we get some money, I want to get my nails done. They'd look nice if they were all like this," she says, pointing to the longest nail, which is on the middle finger of her left hand.

"I'm going to kick his ass if he's out with his friends," Al says.

"How much did you give him?" Donna asks.

"A lot this time."

"You wanna go inside and wait?"

"No," Al says. "This is too important. Besides it's too fucking hot."

"What time is it?"

"Twelve-thirty."

"You give a kid some responsibility," Donna says, "and instead of making the most of it, he fucks it up."

"I'm not going to jump to conclusions," the boy's father says. "He did alright last time."

"How much did he get?"

"Almost fifteen-hundred. Brought me back what he didn't sell, too," Al says.

He throws his empty beer can at a tomcat eating garbage from the gutter. The cat hisses and runs away.

Two cars pull up in front of the building. Six guys jump out and start to fight. Al runs inside to get his gun. Donna stays on the stairs and grabs another beer, trying to open it with a nail that's already broken.

Al comes back out and starts shooting his gun in the air.

"Get the fuck out of here, you punks," he shouts.

The guys jump back in their cars and drive away, throwing bottles at Al as they pull off.

"Some fucking neighborhood," Al says, sitting back down next to his wife, placing the gun beside him. His face is red with anger.

Donna rubs his neck and nuzzles him. He takes his t-shirt off. She runs her nails through his chest hair.

"Go ahead and get your nails done," he says. He puts her fingers in his mouth and sucks them.

At about one, their son, Joe, appears.

"Where you been?" Al asks.

"Selling the stuff like you told me to," Joe says. He is skinny and he looks down at the ground when he talks to his father.

"How much you get?" his father asks him.

"A grand."

Al stands up.

"What? I gave you at least two thousand worth."

"It was a bad night," his son says.

"What do you mean, a bad night? Give me the rest of the shit back."

"I ain't got nothing left. Here's the money."

"Where's the crack, Joe?" Donna asks. She stands up too.

"I got taken once, and I had to sell low just to make a thousand," Joe says, his voice quivering.

"The shit you did," his mother says. "You smoked it."

"I swear," Joe says.

"You and your fucking friends," Donna says. She comes down off the stairs and grabs Joe by the hair. The boy says nothing.

"You're fucking lying," she says.

She kicks him with her bare feet. She scratches his face with her fingernails, slaps him a few times, and knees him the groin. Her halter top has slipped down and one breast is exposed. She does not notice. Joe falls to the ground and she kicks him repeatedly. She pours beer in his face.

"Get in the fucking house," she says. "Get the fuck in the house. I don't want to see you out of your room tomorrow. You hear me?" She is screaming now. Some neighbors have gathered in the doorway.

"What the fuck are you looking at?" she shouts. "Mind your own goddamn business!"

The neighbors leave and Joe gets up off the ground and heads inside. He is pretty scuffed up, but not really hurt, though Donna is a big woman. Joe gets an erection during the scuffle with his mother. He rubs his crotch as he slams shut the door of his room.

With everyone inside, Donna sits down next to Al and takes a sip from her beer.

"I didn't waste it all on that little asshole," she says after a long gulp.

She touches her toenails. They hurt where she kicked Joe, but they did not break.

"I'm going to get a pedicure, too," Donna says. "And I'm going to leave my toenails long. I like them this way."

Al pulls her top up, squeezing her breast before he covers it. She giggles at the thought her tit was hanging out. He starts to rub her thigh.

"You shouldn't beat him so bad," Al says.

"You do much worse, sweetheart," she says. She pushes his hand from her leg.

"Well."

"Al, he's got to mind. You can't trust him. He's no fucking good."

Donna still breathes heavily.

"I agree with you there," Al says.

He puts his hand back on her thigh and slides it up under her denim shorts. She lights another long, brown cigarette. The tomcat reappears at the curb. This time Al does not chase him away. Donna runs her nails along Al's fore-arm. They share her cigarette and open another beer. It is nearly two o'clock and the neighborhood is finally quiet.

Foot Girl

She was begging, barefoot in the rain. Nineteen, maybe twenty. She was sitting on the sidewalk, legs outstretched. Her feet were filthy, but beautiful—high arches, thin ankles. I gave her a dollar, then a ten. My hands were shaking badly.

I took the tube of moisturizer out of my jacket pocket.

"May I massage your feet?"

I sat down beside her. At first she tucked her feet under her thighs, hiding them. I sat next to her silently and waited. Slowly she relaxed and put her legs and feet back out. She flexed and curled her toes. I had nothing to clean her feet with but it didn't matter. I put the cream in my hand, lifted her feet gently, and began to rub.

I need to live near water, but I hate getting wet.

My clothes were soaking by then.

"Do you think I'm crazy?" she asked.

Surrounded by puddles, I massaged her and we kissed blindly and for hours before the cops told us to move on.

Serendipity strikes the right chord. Chick-with-child is almost out of booze.

Pregnant Girl

A tall blonde chick chats me up at the bar. I love tall girls. Not tonight. I'm not interested. I've got my eyes on this pregnant slut sloshing vodka three bar stools over. She's like seven months, eight months, just drinking away.

All they have on tap here is Bud and Bud Light and this watery brew makes me piss like a racehorse. I have no other cliché. It works though. It gives me an excuse to leave Blondie. I take the opportunity. The men's' room is no grosser than most, puddles of piss on the floor. I can never figure why guys can't get it in the bowl. But I'm in a hurry. I'm not sure why. My big-belly girl has been alone all night.

Back from the bathroom, I move four seats down. I still have space. I'm less sure about time.

Serendipity strikes the right chord. Chick-with-child is almost out of booze.

"Can I buy you a drink?" I ask.

"Sure," she says. "Double vodka and soda."

I flag the bartender.

The barkeep does not hesitate. She pours the drink long and hard, maybe a triple if I had to guess.

Preggers rubs her big belly and thanks me.

"How are you?" I ask.

"Shit-faced," she says.

"Can I touch it?" I ask.

"All you want."

I rub her stomach and then I suck her fingers.

Her nails are long and her hair is shiny just like they say in all the books.

She puts one hand on my crotch and kneads my balls like she's in cooking class.

"When are you due?"

"Any time now."

I want to ask her a lot more questions but I don't.

Her long nails are quite dirty and I suck the fingers of the hand that is not stroking me. Within a minute or two, her nails are pink and white and clean. She smiles at me.

She changes hands.

Her drink is gone and I order her another and I get myself a scotch on top of my fourth Bud Light. I consider sipping the scotch but instead I gulp it down and order another.

My girl spasms some and I guess I look alarmed.

She moves her face closer to mine.

"Braxton-Hicks," she says.

"What?"

"False alarm."

I remember the books I read and the classes I took.

We drink our drinks.

The jukebox walks the line, just right, a perfect and automatic DJ in the dark. The beer signs glow. The light is blue and black. The six-foot blonde is playing pool.

All at once the moment works.

Pregnant girl finishes her vodka.

"Take me home," she says.

She stumbles a bit getting off her chair. I steady her, my arm under hers. I pick up her purse from the floor and I hand it to her. I grab my jacket and slip it around her suddenly shivering shoulders.

My heart is beating fast and my face is flushed and I am very hard.

I hold both her hands and lead her to my car.

Death at Night

Jandra said that she was going to go see him and I said that it was dumb and a bad idea, and that you couldn't talk to him when he was like that.

"You're just jealous," she said.

We'd never been a couple, and she never talked to me like that, but, "Suit yourself," I said.

We were standing under a streetlight.

She was shivering.

I was sweating a little.

We were different like that.

Bobby had run off screaming after throwing a drink in her face.

"I'm just going to stop by and see him—kiss and make up—and go home," she said.

A light rain started to fall.

"Do me a favor," I said. "If you're just going to stop by his house, and make nice, then meet me afterwards at PJ's for a nightcap."

"What's the point?"

"It's on your way home."

"You're being paranoid."

"You're taking a chance."

"Or jealous."

"That's crazy and you know it."

"Or both."

"PJ's. Last call's at one-thirty."

"OK, OK."

"See ya."

We stood silent in the drizzle for a moment.

I forget which one of us turned to walk away first.

I went straight to the bar.

Even though I knew a bunch of people who were there, I sat alone on a stool.

A couple of people came up to me.

"Joey, we got a table. Come on over and join us for a beer."

"I'm meeting somebody," I said.

I huddled over my drink.

"You meeting Jandra?"

"Naw," I said.

Bobby was maybe my best friend though I hated his temper.

I'd known Jandra since 8th grade. We spent a lot of time together.

The whole neighborhood hung out at PJ's.

A few more handshakes and pats on the back and they left me alone.

By last call I'd been there about an hour and I'd had four drinks.

Jandra never showed up. No call, no text, nothing.

The place cleared out at two.

I smoked a bowl in the parking lot with Richie.

I kept looking around and side to side.

"Who you looking for?" he asked.

"Ah, nobody. Hey, thanks for the weed, man."

"Good stuff, huh?"

I don't smoke much. Really I was just killing some more time, thinking she might show up late.

"Yeah, really good. Thanks, man."

I hardly ever say "man." I do around Richie. I guess because he's a stoner.

I went home and had a couple of shots of Jack so I could sleep.

The next day, I was hung over and I forgot to take my cell phone to work. It wasn't until I got home that I found out that Jandra was dead and that Bobby had killed her.

Hong Kong Hotel

Everything was green.

I thought I knew what I liked, who I liked.

She couldn't have been more different.

My girlfriend was Asian, under five feet and under a hundred pounds.

This girl, the one across from me, was six-two, maybe taller. She was barefoot and bleach-blonde.

The bar was green—at least the light was.

We were in Hong Kong. I speak Chinese. Apparently our dialects differ—I had no one to talk to.

"I want you really badly," I said to her.

"I'm not sure what you mean," she said.

I didn't expect that answer.

I hesitated and became confused.

I tried to think of a quote—Horace or Seneca or Cicero.

I came up short.

"Arma virumque cano" did not seem to fit the situation.

I stopped searching for the right thing to say.

Instead I said the same thing over.

"I want you really badly."

I was still not sure she understood.

I ordered another drink.

She reached over. I kissed her. She kissed me back. We kissed again and again. I told her again how badly I wanted her.

She left to go to the bathroom. She excused herself politely. She never came back.

I stayed until last call. I had another drink. When the lights came on, I went back up to my room.

Boredom

We were hanging around Gina's house again.

"S'up?"

Jimmy joined us and we smacked hands.

"S'up?"

Tessa lit up a bowl. She passed it around.

Hours went by.

There was a thing on the table and another thing next to it.

Richie had stuff in his pocket and he took it out and looked at it and put it back.

"Grab me a beer?"

After the smoke, Tessa was looking at something out the window.

"S'up tonight?"

"Nothin.'"

I had something on the bottom of my shoe. I picked at it until it came off.

Billy pulled out his cock and started whacking off.

"Hey, don't get spunk on the couch."

He came in his hand.

More hours went by.

I was looking at the floor. There was a lot of random shit on the rug—dust and stuff.

Mostly Gina's place was nice.

She had a job and shit.

There was stuff in the fridge, but not much.

Gina tried to think of something to do.

It got to be three in the morning.

There was nothing to do, but there were things at Gina's apartment, like she had beer and cigarettes, and we drank and we smoked and we popped some pills and shit.

Then it got to be four.

"Wanna go get some chips or something, some smokes, I think I'm running out?"

"Yeah, I want something."

"OK, let's go get something."

Richie and I wanted something to eat, but we weren't sure what.

So we headed out to the store to get something.

"7-11?"

"Yeah."

We headed over there.

Outside, we looked around. There was stuff on the street and other stuff on the sidewalk and it blew around in the gutter and sometimes it landed in doorways or wrapped around telephone poles or mailboxes and shit. We kept walking. We had a ways to go, not far, but like a little bit, before we got to the 7-11.

Inside the 7-11, they had a lot of stuff, shit like Cheetos and Kit Kats and all kinds of shit to drink.

We were gonna get some chips or some shit like Richie said.

They had all kinds of stuff.

We didn't look around much.

Like at the counter, we just stood there and we didn't move around and shit.

We didn't look at shit and we didn't buy shit or steal anything, so we looked straight at the clerk and the clerk just stood there.

No one said shit.

Then Richie just said, "Shit, I don't know," and then he just pulled out a gun and then the motherfucker behind the counter just froze and shit and Richie just didn't say shit, but he pulled the trigger and the guy just fell over, all covered in red, and I think his shirt was white and shit, so it really showed up, but anyway it was all red now and shit.

Still we didn't buy stuff or steal anything; we just left, like walked back outside.

Back at Gina's, we both—Richie and me—just sat back down on the couch, where we were sitting before. Everybody was still there, but there was lots of room. Gina had like a lot of chairs.

"You get chips?"

"No."

"What'dya do?"

"Just took a walk and shit."

"Oh."

Tessa lit another bowl.

She passed it to me and I inhaled a deep lungful of weed and passed it to Richie.

Heroin Chick

"Hey, heroin girl," I said. "What's up?"

She was skinny as fuck, and standing on Hollywood Boulevard, right by the subway station off Vine.

I wanted to fuck her.

We chatted for a while, all small talk.

She didn't have much to say.

Then this lady—she'd been standing there the whole time, like waiting for the bus or something—anyway, she started to convulse.

Heroin chick immediately kicked into action—CPR, resuscitation, whatever it's called, the whole bit. It was amazing; she was amazing.

Meanwhile, I called 911 on my cell phone.

The EMT crew arrived.

Heroin girl backed off.

We started kissing.

A cop wanted to ask her questions.

She talked shit.

The lady seemed OK.

The paramedics took her away.

Everything calmed down.

I led my girl away, into the dark, into the back of the unlit parking lot opposite the Pantages.

We continued to kiss. We kissed more and more.

The she said, "Hey, hey, just a minute, we gotta stop, just for a minute."

She fumbled in her purse.

She found what she was looking for.

She tied off; she shot up.

She couldn't really kiss anymore.

That was it.

Interlude

Adeste Fidelis

Beyond Denver

Just as the sun set the Shoshone man pulled the trigger.

Earlier in the day a cop had killed his brother.

By nightfall he had fulfilled his promise to his family by shooting the policeman.

The moonless sky made the oncoming night particularly dark.

The Shoshone threw the gun in the dumpster, but his disposal of the weapon would prove to be of no use.

Leaving Beijing

We take the train out of Beijing.

My girlfriend is young.

It is our first time in China.

We chortle through the city and out of it.

"I want to take your picture," Cheryl says to me.

She kisses me, then rifles through her purse.

"My camera's gone!"

"Are you sure?"

"It was in my purse."

"Did you put your purse down?"

"When I couldn't find my ticket."

"It's so fucking crowded. Somebody must have reached in and grabbed it."

"Maybe it just fell out."

"We should tell somebody."

"It won't do any good."

"Maybe somebody found it, not stole it."

"They're still gonna keep it. It doesn't have my name on it."

"You never know."

"We don't speak Chinese."

"Someone will speak English."

"I'm not upset about it," Cheryl says.

I believe her, but I tell the conductor anyway.

It seems like the right thing to do.

It can't hurt.

The train ride is not smooth.

Cheryl's red roots show beneath the deep black she has dyed her hair.

I kiss her high forehead.

**

They stop the train. They make us get off.

"This can't be about my camera?"

"They wouldn't stop the train for that. It must be something big."

"Scary."

"Yeah, a little nerve-wracking."

The police search everybody but us.

When they apprehend the man they think that did it, they remove him from the train.

Alongside the tracks, as we all watch, four uniformed officials draw their pistols and shoot the man dead.

Heroes

Ad Majorum Dei Gloriam

(A.M.D.G.)

Repatriation

He returned from Iraq. He stood by the gate of the army base. No one came to pick him up. Several busses passed by. He watched them come and go. Finally he boarded a bus. He was going home to Los Angeles.

The afternoon was very hot. At the Greyhound Terminal on Cahuenga he got confused. His address was on his driver's license: 1106 East Pico Boulevard #203. He decided to walk.

When he got to his apartment, his wife was there. He could tell because her car was parked out front. Same car.

He climbed the stairs to the 2nd floor. He knocked on the door.

"Remember me?" he asked.

"Yes," she said.

She kissed him and let him inside.

He dropped his duffel bag and looked around.

"Looks the same," he said.

"I painted the place," she said.

"Looks nice," he said.

It was already nightfall.

Outside gang members started shooting their guns.

He tried not to flinch.

"Where's our son?"

"In foster care," she said.

He did not react.

She handed him a beer and opened one for herself. Miller Genuine Draft.

He'd been gone eighteen months.

Sitting on the couch they drank two more beers—the front door open, the heavy metal screen door closed against the bugs and the bullets.

He noticed a Bible on the coffee table.

"You get religious?" he asked.

"I've been praying," she said.

He re-arranged a vase of plastic flowers poised next to the Bible.

They talked sparsely for a while longer. An hour went by.

"Will you sleep with me?" he asked.

"Yes," she said.

He closed and locked the door.

He took her on the couch.

He fucked her fast and furious.

When he released his hands from around her neck, his cum shot deep inside her, she was definitely cold and lifeless and very dead.

Be All You Can Be

I returned from Fallujah in March of 2005. I'd been shot, but not badly hurt, and I was still in the Army.

They assigned me to recruitment. I worked at an office in Glendale, California, next to a place called Zankou Chicken. Zankou Chicken was popular, and a lot of people came there. Most days I had chicken or falafel for lunch, always with a side of hummus. The pita bread was warm and good and comforting. At the time, I did not have a girlfriend.

Every day, I signed up recruits. Most were Latino; some were Armenian. The newspapers reported the casualties every day. Some of the men and women who came by my desk were scared; some had no other choices.

One morning, early, two brothers came in. Twins, as it turned out. I asked them a lot of questions. Both wanted to enlist.

"What does your mother think of your idea?" I found myself asking them.

At our training sessions, we were told never to ask that question. They even showed us a memo from the Assistant Undersecretary of the Army. Some mucky-muck.

I sent the two boys home.

A couple of days later, some local bigwigs called me in for consultations.

I had violated policy.

I was given two weeks leave without pay. A slap on the wrist.

They had no interest in having our recruitment tactics find their way into the press.

The first day I was back at my desk, another set of twins came in to enlist. Without so much as a hiccup, I signed them both on the dotted line.

No Zankou Chicken that day. I sent out for lunch. Chinese food. Fifteen minute express delivery to my door. I'd made my quota for the month. The Army would be paying me a bonus.

I stood up again and
lit another cigarette.

An Insurrection

A new rebellion had started up. Bombs dropped like birds shot from the sky. They shelled us for three days. Then it started to rain.

The wind came up strong for a bit, then stopped.

The girl was running in the rain, without a headscarf.

I smoked a cigarette in the doorway of the remains of a building—sheer walls intact, all else gone.

I could see her hair, snaggled in the wind. She was barefoot. I fall in love with barefoot women.

I had a bad feeling. I wanted to protect her. I could have sworn her eyes were green.

My mother had green eyes. My mother died while I was stationed here. I got a an email and a call.

The girl ran slow, then faster, then slow again.

I think she was out of breath.

I stepped from the doorway where I was smoking.

I told myself I was in love.

I threw my cigarette butt out into the driving rain.

I shouted at the running girl.

I shouted, "Hey!"

I began to run out to her, into the street, out of my doorway.

My platoon leader, my friend, grabbed me by the shoulder. I hit him in the face and I tried to run.

He was bigger than me; he wrestled me to the ground. I was pinned to the ground by him and by another soldier.

I could see my cigarette butt, wet and snuffed in the hard rain.

The shots from a rooftop—I'm not sure which one, not that it matters—cut the girl down quickly. The shots were many. She fell first forward, then back. Like JFK, I think.

My friends let me up off the ground.

I made to run to her.

They tossed me back to the pavement.

They let me go again.

I stood up again and lit another cigarette.

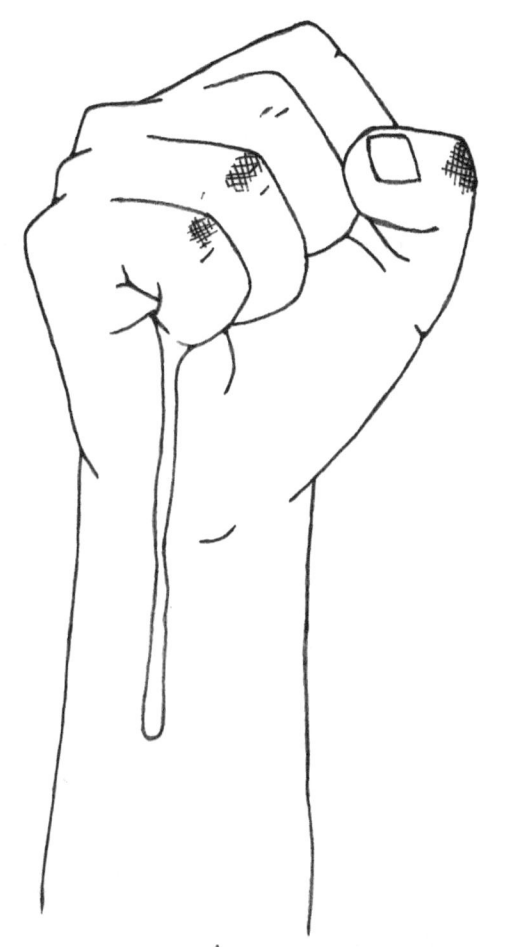

My dick gets real hard
when I hit people.

The Common Inquisitor

I beat the shit out of them.

That's what I do.

I'm proud of what I do.

I like my work.

I'm happy to oblige.

I love my job.

I'd like to say I'm just following orders, but that would be a lie. I do not lie.

I can say I am patriotic, but that's only a half-truth. Because it's not the main reason I do what I do.

I like busting teeth more than I like getting laid. And I love to fuck. It's Number Two on my list.

My dick gets real hard when I hit people.

I get paid to proffer violence, which is great. A government issue paycheck. I've never had to do some boring day job. I know I am a lucky man.

They bring the cocksuckers in. They won't talk. They sing like songbirds when I'm through with them.

There's some shit-talk we get bad information. That's fucking bullshit. These pricks don't dare lie to me.

Fuck the *Washington Post* and all those limp-wristed pieces of shit.

When I get my fist down some sand nigger's throat, and I'm about to rip his goddamn lungs out with my bare hands, he don't fucking lie.

I guarantee you.

I'm not ignorant; I know my history. I know about Torquemada. I've studied his moves, his methods. A Dominican priest, after all. How great is that? I admire that motherfucker. The Spanish kicked some serious ass back then, didn't they?

Sometimes I think the whole fucking country is going soft. The autoworkers whine; the stockbrokers whine. Lehman Brothers went out of business. Who gives a shit? Fuck the hardhats and fuck the boys from Gucci Gulch.

My tour of duty is up in six months. One-hundred-eighty days to kick ass under color of authority. Then I'm free to be a badass. I signed on with a private contractor. Assigned to all that rendition kind of shit. I can't wait.

Free at last, free at last, thank God Almighty, I am free at last!

Demons

Everything looked febrile red and burnt orange. Twenty minutes, tops, before sundown.

The man scampered along the rubble, then cowered amidst it. He wore no shirt and his face and arms and hands were cut and bloody and bleeding still. I slammed him between the shoulders with my rifle butt. He fell face forward.

"You fuck!" I shouted at his prostrate back.

I spat on the back of his head as I got ready to kick him.

Two soldiers restrained me from behind.

**

For the past four days the explosions had assumed a rhythm—at nine at noon and at three every day—destruction in three-quarter time. The air was filled with shredded matter, a haze in the dry wind, a violent and unnatural entropy, disorder arriving much too quickly and much too soon.

I arrived in country as a scientist, albeit one with military rank.

My degrees, my doctorate, had all become irrelevant. My past was anger now; my future rage.

**

When the soldiers let me go I went after the man again. They restrained me again; this time they led me away.

"Leave me alone!" I swung my arms. They knocked me down, picked me up, hauled me to the car, and shoved me into the backseat, doorlocks clicking from the front.

We drove off fast, first on pavement, then on dirt, then on pavement again.

"Fucking child safety locks!" I shouted, futilely trying the door over and over again.

"You're fucking losing it."

"He fucking did it."

"He didn't fucking do shit."

"He did. He's fucking guilty as fuck."

"*He* didn't do it."

"They did. All of them did. He fucking did it."

"He didn't fucking do it."

**

We had left the man alone among the rubble, with the rubble, in the rubble. As rubble. Like rubble. Blameless, struck no more, but there by himself. (A man unfamiliar with Beckett, but waiting for Godot nonetheless.)

We drove a long way, due west, from that man, and we had left him even farther behind than that. I remember the sun set hard and quick that night like a pistol shot, almost instantaneously, the red and the orange suddenly gone black, visible no longer. Like people and things, colors yield, give way, die, disappear.

Confrontation

The blows came first to my face then to my body. The music they played was strange. Someone said the band was Australian. Girls and highways. Power chords. At high volume, very loud. I grew up in Chicago. They made fun of my name. When the naked woman came to my cell, I professed my values. In truth, I thought she was cute. I would never say. Honestly she was not strong. Her hits increased my resolve. Her fingernails were dirty. That's what I remember. She turned the lights on much brighter. I closed my eyes. I would not disclose my fantasies. As she struck me I hid my joy and my shame. I had never left the country. That is the truth. I went to New York once. When I was a boy. My father lives there. He did not come back with us to Chicago. I tell her I like the wind. She does not understand. Her skinny arms swing her whip again. My face shows no pain. A male soldier punches me. I am not so fond of that. I describe my time in Los Angeles. I have never been there. Skateboards on the boardwalk and letters on the walls. They turn the music up. Up to this point, I shed no blood. Now my nose is broken. Then my jaw. The girl did it. She dropped her stick and her whip. She struck me with her fist. I like her still. I strained against the ropes and handcuffs. I want to be with her. They left me alone with the noise and the light. I could not sleep. She came back to kick me. I try to pucker my lips but my jaw and my face are broken. She kicks me again. I can hear and feel my ribs crack. The rest of them come back. They tape my nose and mouth. It is now and it is then. They throw me on the floor. I try to tell their boots apart, hers from theirs. I cannot. They kicked me all at once. She would have smaller shoes, but their kicks were rapid and hard to tell apart. Their shoes were all the same. Blindfolded I could not tell if she was naked any more, nor if she ever was. Their sounds went away, the noise of their boots stuttering away from me. Some time later, soft sounds return. I cannot rise from the floor. What seems to be a small boot presses against my throat. I think I hear her voice. A bit of pressure against my windpipe, then a little more. I cough and gag under the weight of her foot. I have nothing to say to them, nothing to tell her.

At Play

The mortar shells often fell just outside the house—in the yard, in the street, just beyond the neighbor's door.

Khaled loved to play outdoors.

When his mother caught him outside, she would scold him and send him in to sit alone, to contemplate, to pray—without playing—to think it over.

"It is dangerous out there," she said.

Khaled was seven. His sister Laila was ten. Rangina, their mother, was thirty-five.

"Watch out for him," she told her daughter.

The streets were all of dirt and very dirty, carpets of garbage and things discarded, refuse left behind. Khaled liked to play with the trash, with the disposed objects—with cans and boxes and with old tools and utensils.

He was a good boy and he was seven.

One day the earth rumbled and the house shook.

Mother and daughter had been cooking together.

Rangina grabbed her daughter's hand and started for the door.

"Khaled! Khaled!" the mother shouted.

She and Laila looked around the small house.

The earthquake was large and the structure was clearly giving way.

"He must be playing outside," Laila said.

The pair ran out the door.

Indeed, Khaled had been playing outside. But when the rumbling started, he became afraid of getting in trouble. He assumed the racket was the gunfire and the shelling that his mother had warned him about.

He made it back inside just as the house collapsed.

Repatriation II

Steven sat in the front row when Secretary Rumsfeld addressed the troops in Baghdad.

"You are American heroes. The entire nation is in your debt."

During Rumsfeld's remarks, Steven started to well up. So did the soldier sitting beside him.

Steven had his mother keep all the newspapers though his picture was never in them. But he was there.

At the corner of Fifth and Figueroa, in the heart of financial LA, Steven shouted hoarsely:

"I'm a fucking hero. Wait! Wait! They're going to shoot me. Help me! Help me! The train is off the track. You're a motherfucking raccoon."

The bankers and the lawyers, the clerks and the secretaries, all waited for the "Walk" sign to cross the streets. The traffic signals both flashed and beeped. Light covered light. The sun was straight overhead at noon and at lunch.

"Fuck you, you fucking bum," a man in a blue suit shouted straight in Steven's face.

Roadside

There are trees and there is green and there is trash and there are stray dogs. People cannot afford their dogs here and they let them go.

There is concrete and asphalt.

The dogs wander the streets like my dreams.

Roadside bombs. I wonder too what that means. I should know.

I think of roadside diners and roadside attractions—HoJo's and Denny's, and places called Connie's, outlet stores and haunted houses, farmers at wooden stands selling peaches and cherries, the Painted Desert, and dinosaurs outside Palm Springs.

I think of places I want to be.

**

I roll up to the Slauson exit off the 110.

I wonder: "What the fuck am I doing in this neighborhood?"

I make less money overall, but the motorists are nicer. It's much better than downtown. And the Westside is worse.

I am hungry for pizza, but I can't even find a Little Caesar's.

I settle for a quarter-pounder.

They don't like my wheelchair at the McDonald's drive-thru. They laugh at me.

The girl at the first window—the one where I order—is tiny and cute. Mayan perhaps. I can't be sure. Indian anyway.

She does not find me handsome. I can tell.

When the shouting begins at the next window, I want to fight.

I cannot fight.

I watch and wait.

In my motorized wheelchair, I am a roadside attraction.

**

IED's. Improvised Explosive Devices. Now that sounds better. More scientific, more serious. They're all over the news. You ever try to take one of those things apart? To disarm it? To follow orders, to do your duty, to perform the job you were trained to do, were told to do?

**

I wear a medal. Saint Christopher. The patron saint of travelers. My mother gave it to me. Some say now that he is not a saint; maybe he never existed. I don't believe them.

**

The Community Redevelopment Agency paid for this shopping center—the PayLess Shoes, the wig store, the nail salon, the Fallas Paredes store, a Taco Bell, this McDonald's where I wait for my burger and fries.

At the second window, a different cute girl hands me my food. I give her my cash.

Her fake fingernails—long with French tips—flash in the fluorescent light. I eat my hamburger and drink my soda in the handicapped parking space.

Booted out and moved along by the McDonald's manager, and back at the Slauson offramp, I jiggle my cup. Shaken vigorously, the melting ice sounds like spare change, like my fortune, like my roadside future. I have earned three dollars.

Just Outside the Green Zone

We were supposed to be doing something else, patrolling I suppose. Things are never/seldom clear.

Instead we were fucking in a hotel room, paid in full by American taxpayers.

"Scratch me!"

She tore at me with her fingernails.

"Harder!"

She dug in, broke my skin, drew blood.

Her nails didn't break. They only did more and more damage. She slapped me and started to scream. I egged her on.

There were empty liquor bottles, some broken, scattered all around the room.

The air conditioner barely worked. It was hot as shit.

We fucked and fucked.

We were both slathered in sweat.

I was bloody; she was not.

I wanted to be smothered in her authority.

She pissed in my mouth.

She clenched my cock tight with her fingernails.

I came again, hard into her hand.

She came again too as my cock bled onto her fingers.

I was pleased I had drawn out her cruelty. She didn't like my smugness. I guess it showed. Her nails weren't that long, maybe a quarter-inch, but they were sharp as hell. She raked my face so everyone would see.

She screamed more and slapped me more, her face flushed red.

We figured out later that the bomb had gone off in the lobby café.

Our room was on an upper floor.

We could still hear all the noise. We were supposed to do something, help with the evacuation, whatever.

She stopped screaming.

I looked at her—half-heartedly waiting for orders. Her face was less red.

She slapped me, somewhat softly this time.

We had one more bottle of bourbon on the nightstand.

She shoved it in my face.

"Open it!"

The deep red returned to her skin.

I worked on the wax bottle cap with my teeth.

Later we straightened the room out the best we could.

We used the emergency exit to leave. We avoided altogether the mayhem on the ground floor.

Fuck Him

I saw the whole thing.

    He tossed a grenade, a bomb of some kind.

    I saw it.

    I know it was him.

    I have him against a wall, my gun at his head.

    My sergeant shouts, "No!!!"

    I close my eyes.

    I see my girlfriend's tits, small, but lovely.

    The sergeant shouts again.

    I pull the trigger anyway.

    Dust is dust.

Re-assigned

"I'm gonna fuck you, then shoot you, or the other way around. So then I'll fuck you after you're dead and you won't even know, but that doesn't seem as much fun... You understand?"

"Cocksucker!"

"Oh shit, I'm sorry."

"You can't talk. Why? Because I knocked your teeth out and broke your jaw."

"You're in pain? I'm so sorry. Fuck you, you piece of shit."

"Oh shit, wait. You have two hands. I think I'll cut one off. Sever it. Throw it in the trash."

"Maybe, I'll fucking eat it."

"Okay, so this is a one-way conversation. I get it. I love one-way conversations."

"You feel that? That's my boot on your balls. Can I crush them? No children for you. Yes, I can. Si, se puede. Crunch, crunch. No more testicles. Just mush."

"Where are we?

"You came—ha, ha—on a plane."

"I think you're in Bulgaria or Romania. Some horseshit East European country—It doesn't matter"

"Who gives a shit?"

* *

Torture talk is always fun—The euphemisms are pure gold—extraordinary rendition.

Who came up with that? They should get a medal.

Torture was my second assignment.

"Is this a confession?" you ask.

Categorically not.

It is a tale of pride and glee.

* *

Back then, I was naive.

"What do we do?"

"Just fucking shoot," he said.

They said they were inside mud huts.

What the fuck?

They looked like mud huts to me

Some assholes were paddling a boat.

"Open fire."

It was cool how they popped out of their seats when they got shot, the oars flaying from their hands under the full moon.

Fucking shitholes I never hear of—Falluja, Haditha, Tikrit.

I got my ass promoted.

All I could promise was death.

"Slow and painful," I always said.

These pussies were freaked out, scared, sad, same shit.

Are you fucking kidding me?

Sad about what?

Some shitbirds in rowboats?

Towelheads in tents?

That's just bullshit.

Mercy is just not in my job description.

Some motherfuckers crawled out of a shack.

These other guys, they hesitated.

Fuck that.

I pulled the trigger.

It's easier to shoot the fuckers when they're on their hands and knees.

They sent this bitch in from Bagdad. Had her take photos.

"Can I feel your tits?"

She had nice big tits.

"You wanna help?" I asked. We need more body bags.

The cradle of civilization, my ass.

"This one's a teenager."

"Who gives a shit?"

The *Washington Post* is always looking for excuses for a guy like me. Like maybe my sister got raped back home and that's why I'm so angry. Or they've pegged someone like me. Because they don't know me—Like, personally, I mean."

"It's just some more horseshit.

I don't even have a sister.

I just have a job to do and I do it well.

Beginning of story, end of story.

But not this story.

My tale is ongoing.

It continues, it goes on. It does not end. Here in Bucharest now. I love this city, this special place where I've got this guy in my clutches who I'm just gonna kill.

Peacekeeper

The nun was watching both of us.

She had been sent by an international relief agency.

It was cold, much colder than I was used to. I had lived in California for a long time, in Los Angeles.

Now I was a United Nations peacekeeper.

The other captive was our captor's enemy. I was neutral. The nun was there to make sure there were no atrocities. Our captor did not care about the nun.

He handed me a knife.

He pointed at his enemy and he looked at me.

"Peacekeeper, stab him right now or I will shoot both of you," he said.

I declined.

The captor shrugged.

He made the same proposition to his enemy, that he should kill me or we both would die. Though we had never spoken, the other man, our captor's enemy, refused as well.

Our captor then shot the nun.

"You didn't say anything about the nun," the enemy of our captor said.

The captor then shot him.

I braced myself.

"Keep the peace," the captor said and then he walked away, leaving me with the corpses of his enemy and the nun.

I sat there and shivered in the cold with the two dead bodies.

Drones

Always is not forever. All the time is not forevermore, nor never-ending. I am doodling. Perhaps I am writing greeting cards. God knows, I need a hobby.

**

They deliver to me an ergonomic chair—leather seat, chrome backing, pinioned wheels, dials and levers for adjustment of position. A fine instrument, perfectly engineered.

I sit at a desk.

In my ear: Bose noise-filtering headphones. I prefer not to talk, nor to listen.

My iPod: Radiohead, Sigur Ros, a bit of Bjork, more Radiohead. I need atmosphere.

On screen: encryption, confirmation, code, correction, finalization.

I download songs from iTunes; I order books from Amazon; I am ordered otherly, otherwise.

Images indistinct, blurrier than thought; yet I am certain.

Inchoate; ineluctable. I think of words.

Inaction: the waiting period.

I turn my music up. In volume.

Remote: they are remote; I am remote. Remote region, desolate landscape.

Next: a blizzard of communication, complicated confirmation.

Hours go by.

Dinner deferred.

Deployment successful.

My skills are valued!

I do not read the papers.

I do not watch the news.

At the end of a long day, I stop for beer and go home alone.

**

Alone is not lonely.

I have my dreams.

Green Eyes

Her coat is huge, way too big for her.

Her eyes are green.

That's all I can tell, all I can see.

She comes at me with open arms, as if for an embrace.

I love her eyes.

Concrete, rebar, reinforced, Isabella, saxophone, sailing ships. Ornaments of the world.

I want to hug her, to kiss her, to fuck her.

She tells me to get away.

I know what is underneath her fabric.

I imagine her skin.

She is not wearing shoes.

Her feet are coffee and beautiful, just below her hemline.

I no longer make eye contact.

She opens her jacket. It is all there—wire and grenades; her breasts are bare.

Winds blow; sand stings my skin; she hesitates.

So do I.

Our language is not the same.

We feel the air.

There are the sniper's bullets.

Upended, she is down.

Detainees

I am not supposed to talk to her.

    She cannot talk to me.

    The wind is now to nil.

    Guards watch us.

**

The German girl at the hotel had a camera.

    At first I was shy.

    Then I was indiscreet.

    I hammed before her tripod.

    I sobered up.

    Our antics now made me nervous.

    I nearly had to break her arm to destroy the pictures.

**

Sand has always annoyed me. I've never liked the beach. As a child, on sum-

115

mer vacations, I would stay on the boardwalk—concrete, asphalt; wooden piers, OK, just not sand.

Here I am now in a war that is nothing but sand.

Sculpted, winded. Knocked about.

Drinking coffee carries threats. Explosions rampant.

Unclarity; some things certain.

**

I outrank the guards. Not by much, but still.

I walk by her, brush her lightly.

Her eyes blink rapidly; that's all I can tell.

She turns to face me, as it were.

"Sergeant," I say.

"Captain," the lead guard says.

The girl turns away from me.

The detention center lights are so fluorescent, the walls so white. Glare. Squint. My eyes nearly as shrouded as hers.

I motion a private conference with the guards.

Moments later, I am at the wheel of a Humvee and the girl is my passenger.

I am sure to face a court martial, maybe worse.

**

Red darkness descends.

I flash ID.

We glide through checkpoints.

I really miss my sister.

We kiss in my dreams.

Her name is Emily. She loves the beach. She is three years older. She loves to tease me with the sand between her toes.

I turn to my passenger.

"Do you speak English?"

"A little."

"Do you know where we're going?"

"I'm a Kurd."

We drive outside Baghdad, then back into it.

My gas gauge nears empty.

I lust her brown fingers, her perfect nail beds.

Veiled, she is otherwise invisible.

**

Shelling occurs in the hills. Both distant and near.

"Do you?" "Are you?" I think, but do not ask.

She drops her outer cloak onto the vehicle floor.

I recite Isaiah in my head: "But we are all as an unclean thing, and all our righteousnesses are as filthy rags; and we all do fade as a leaf; and our iniquities, like the wind, have taken us away." (Isaiah 64:6)

Silversun Pickups run in my mind, my own private iPod.

She wears no wire.

**

Stateside: The bouncer asks me to leave.

"Not without her," I say.

"She does not want to be with you," he says.

**

At the Hotel Ishtar, I am awkward.

"I have no problem with your clothing…"

She does not speak.

"I can check you in here…"

Her eyes aim at me; her eyes do not blink.

"…under a different name…"

She does not look like my sister, but my sister is not here, is not coming here.

"What's your name?"

"Kerzi."

"My sister is Emily."

"Emily," she says.

"I have her clothes."

Things must change.

They do, they do.

"You are Emily," I say.

"Yes," she says.

We check in without incident. Roger and Emily Harris. A couple, not brother and sister.

"Are you hungry?"

She nods her head.

"Room service?"

She shakes her head.

At the hotel restaurant she looks lovely in my sister's clothes.

I order wine without asking.

Not surprisingly, she drinks with lust and gusto.

Emily's shirt is tight on her. Her breasts are pressed and pushed close together. I avert my eyes.

**

Back upstairs, she is short in stature. I kiss the top of her head.

"It is better for you if I leave now," I say.

She looks a certain way in my sister's high-fashion jeans.

She falls forward and I catch her. I keep her upright.

We hold one another, then we part company.

I worry about phrasing. Perhaps needlessly.

"You have what you need," I say.

"Are you OK?" she asks.

Silence.

"Will you be?" she says.

"I am good," I say. "I am well."

In her Western clothes, she kisses both my cheeks.

"You should lock the door when I leave," I say.

I hear the deadbolt latch behind my back.

Darkness Drops

You are dead, my love.

That I know.

I am supposed to radio in. I do not.

I stay with you in the shrub and the sand. I stroke your hair. Your hair does not stiffen.

**

We ran for the truck. We almost made it. When the bullets hit you, I scorned the hands that reached out for me. The hands of our fellow soldiers. I scorned them to be with you.

We fell in love at boot camp. We laughed amidst sweat and pondered our prospects. From North Carolina, steamy and wet, to Texas heat to arid Iraq. I stole your shampoo. We believed that no one knew about us.

Time passed here, the invasion easy, the aftermath troubled, letters home, your embrace, still furtive, glancing, clandestine. A game of soccer in the scattered sand.

**

I do not know how to sleep with a dead body, but I am determined to do so. The sun falls. I shape the sand beside you, beneath you. I feel the hot but cooling grit between my fingers.

My radio cackles. I ignore it. At least it's still working, functioning, alive. I banish the thought.

Darkness drops. I crawl up beside you. We talk.

I believe we will talk all night, but at the outset, I am surprised by how little I have to say.

All curled up I have profound things to say to you—about the endurance of love, about morality and ethics, about sacrifice and beautiful suffering, about natural law and various theories of just war, about us.

We both were church-goers.

I say none of this of course.

"Do you remember when I first cut your hair?...you know how I fumble with things...I still can't believe that eggs made you gag..." I confuse my tenses.

The darkness deepens and the wind picks up. I cuddle your corpse. Like a sodden bag of Early Grey, you are steeped in liquid, but yours is blood. Holding death so close, so tightly, the deep shit seems like mere pretense now. In the end, after the end, it is the quotidian that counts.

I see your socks and shoes.

Once again, I take out my radio, or whatever it is I am supposed to call it now, this sophisticated communications device, my MBITR. I think of smashing it, of stomping it into the sand. Instead I stick it—still croaking with static—back inside my jacket, and I hold you, and I wait for morning.

Guns

He started with birds. Things that fall from the sky. Like rain. Or snow. Bombs. Or dead birds.

His aim improves.

Always he gets better at things. Not worse.

She tells him these things.

Back when.

Sand outside Fallujah. Phantom Fury.

And wind.

A kiss on the cheek.

Back then.

Now a man runs across a road.

Kill time.

He fires. The old man falls. A round of applause.

An old woman runs towards the dead man.

What the fuck?

He shoots again.

Another one down.

Laughs. More cheers.

Repeat. Do it again!

We're having fun now.

Billings is the county seat of Yellowstone County. MSU Billings enrolls more than 5000 students.

He once was one of them.

Sand kicks up when the body drops.

She always mumbled.

"Hey, there goes another one."

With the sun where it is, looking west is too hard.

Big breasted bartender serves
me another. Five drinks in,
I am still un-fucked up.

Cross Dressing

I want to drink alone.

I admire the bartender's tits, large and low-slung.

I manage to have three bourbons before the intrusion.

An unshaven man sits beside me. Unkempt, he has a story.

The jukebox plays un-loud.

The guy starts talking: "We just smoked them."

I order another whiskey.

"I got to say, the raghead chick was fine. I'd never fucked a sand nigger before."

At the pool table, this girl has the kind of perfect ass that comes from sitting on a barstool—spread-wide and beautiful.

"You got to get some benefit from serving over there, don't you think?"

"Makes sense," I mumble.

The place is cash only. I check my wallet. I have plenty.

"We had to kill them after we fucked them, you know what I mean?"

I look at my drink.

The lights blink.

I take a notebook from my jacket pocket and I begin to write.

"Hey, you writing about me? I got some stories…"

Barstool chick is good at pool. She laughs and coughs. I imagine her speaking voice.

"You ever do a tour?" the scruffy man asks.

"No," I lie.

My girl was Kuwaiti, twelve years ago, a time of restraint.

"We had no choice," the guy says, drawing close to my face.

Big-breast bartender serves me another.

Five drinks in, I am still un-fucked up.

Shaggy-guy's breath stinks.

I get up to play pool.

Beard-boy stays at the bar. I don't think he can stand.

A scuffle starts at the pool table.

I failed to write my name on the chalkboard.

I have to wait to play.

I sit back down.

I want no more story.

I think of 8th Grade: "Arma virumque cano."

"We strangled them all," he says. "Minimizes evidence."

I do not speak.

"No trip up the river," he says.

At last it is my turn to play pool.

Barfly chick is my opponent.

"Bet?" she asks. Her voice is low and scratchy. Perfect.

"You take me home if I win?"

"Ha!"

The felt on the table is fucked up.

She wins handily anyway.

"Consolation?" I ask.

"What?" I wish she would talk more.

"Walk me to my car?"

"Are you serious?"

"Yes," I say.

I turn to look towards the bar.

Un-razored man narrates to another.

I leave the bar for good.

I look over my shoulder for the name of the place.

I am out of luck.

I talk to myself all the way home.

(Shit out of luck.

It's a prosody I'm looking for.

I can never end things.)

Debaser

The forsaken prison is clearly closed but the door is locked—from the inside. It rattles. A store-bought padlock it would seem. In the stinging heat, we bash it in with rifle butts.

Sand and trash like wind-made sculptures in the dirty corridors; the fetid smell of urine and bile baked at 100 degrees. We hold our breath as best we can.

Guns drawn, we move with care along the row of doorless cells—empty, vacant, abandoned, shattered glass and aged blood stains. Torn shreds of the dictator's portrait flutter in the hot breeze then fall back to the filthy floor.

A wailing arises like a sound from St. John the Divine. Me, I believe even in the Apocrypha.

A soldier fires his gun. I slap it out of his hands.

Inside a wall-less cell an old man sits, emaciated, screaming every thirty seconds like clockwork, his cries punctuated by an equal period of silence.

"My home is here; I will not leave," our interpreter says he is saying. The translator is probably wrong, but close enough.

A soldier hands the old man a canteen of water; the man refuses to take a drink, refuses even to touch the canteen. He shakes his head with vigor.

The impulse to rescue is base and selfish. Not noble as people like to think. Sentimentality is mere ignoble shit.

I look at the man.

I unholster my pistol.

He smiles and nods his head.

I smile back at him in Holy Communion.

I put the barrel of my gun to his forehead and I pull the trigger.

All is well now.

Don't Ask, Don't Tell

We sit in a café.

The coffee is strong.

You are unarmed.

The wind blows hard and the waiter closes the door.

"Hercules," you say.

I raise my eyebrows, silent.

You understand me.

"The wind is strong, the waiter is stronger," you say.

I understand you.

"I must," you say.

"I know," I say.

"Do you?" she asks.

I try to hide that her remark has hurt me.

She starts to speak again.

I put my finger to my lips.

Unmistaken, she draws her body across the table, and—unveiled—she kisses my lips.

Sand straddles our table. The waiter was not quick enough.

I return her kiss.

She leaves and I order another coffee. I linger a while and I read a thick book by Felipe Fernandez-Armesto, a history of the world. Night crashes quickly, crescendos to darkness, like the clap and bang of a falling bomb. I return to my barracks.

The Wagner morning comes suddenly. Neither night nor day can last. Despite the dust, I can see clearly from the compound window. In the mile or so that separates us, the uprooted air lifts matter, dark and real, dead and alive, heavenward like the Ascension. The dawn is punctuated. I make the sign of the cross and I speak aloud in Latin: "In nomine Patris, et Filii, et Spiritus Sancti." I fall silent as the base alarm sounds full alert. I fall to my knees. I rise again within seconds as I am called, with my company, to the scene.

Miniature America: Death Notice

First they threw him in a ditch, then they shot him, or perhaps they shot him first, then threw him in a ditch.

I don't know for sure.

Repatriation III

He checked the ceiling fixture. It could hold his weight. He uncoiled the cord of rope and wrapped it two or three times around the track light rail, taut and tight.

**

The bomb had gone off in the basement. We had been eating oatmeal. First thing in the morning. Suddenly everything exploded, the group of soldiers caught unaware. Telling jokes and stories. Making memories. Wholly unprepared.

Dried blueberries cured in sulfur. Still in the bag. Oatmeal without fruit—a shattered still life when the bomb tore through.

A long tradition in the history of art: the still life. Accurate and realist and cubist and abstract.

Breakfast was fucked and Babcock was dead.

A single dead man.

No others.

But enough. One too many.

**

He had put the light fixtures up all by himself. He had drilled the holes and secured the screws. Home Depot had all the right parts. They had plans and instructions. The whole kit and caboodle. It wasn't just the track lights. He'd made his place a jewel.

Girls came by but he could never sleep. They admired his apartment.

He always had a headache.

He could never fuck.

**

His construction work was sound and solid.

The night was alone.

The rope did not break.

Whore of Babylon

I am a soldier's wife

I haven't seen my husband in two years.

At first, when he left, I watched the news. It was always on, the war, that is.

Now it has fallen from grace. Is that the right way to put it?

I've been seeing a lot of Bernie Madoff lately.

A bit about Karzai and the Afgan election. And Balloon Boy.

Money is tight. The checks are regular, but small.

I don't turn the television on much anymore.

**

I was just sitting at the bar. Three dollar beer, PBR, but what the fuck?

The guy sat next to me.

"What are you drinking?" He asked.

I looked down at my drink. "What does it look like?"

I didn't want to talk to anybody.

"Do you like scotch?"

"Sure, who doesn't?"

"This place is a shithole, but they have a good one here."

"Okay."

He ordered two Glenlivits.

I asked for another PBR, back.

I could tell he approved.

* *

The wheel bent on my daughter's bike. She had pedaled on a bridge. It was beyond repair.

Rain came and we went inside.

She loves "Ramona the Pest" and I read it to her.

The rain stops, but I cannot sleep. It rains again and it rains all night.

* *

"Let's get a pitcher!"

We order a little scotch and a lot of beer.

"I have to pee." I get up from the stool.

"Can you hold it?" He grips my arm quite tightly.

We drive fast to his apartment.

He gets what he wants.

**

Turkey and dressing and lace.

My uncle pukes on the couch. Dead fish float in a bowl. Landscapes and yard sales.

"Is it off balance?" My aunt asks.

Tip the tea—green, black, rosehips, chamomile.

The girl's twelve-year-old ass is naked. We are related.

Tropical fruit—mangoes, guava, papaya.

My napkin is a three-cornered hat.

My nipples are pierced and infected.

* *

My daughter has a new bicycle. Pink and stardust and streamers.

Pizza delivered, with peppers and pepperoni.

Bills paid. No new. No life.

"I drink a lot of beer. My husband is still overseas, at war."

Lynddie

I want you so badly. I want to crawl at your feet. I want you to put a collar around my neck. I want you to lead me on a leash, me on my hands and knees. I want you to whip me.

I have your pictures on my wall. I have enlarged magazine photos into posters, so you loom large over me. I have 300 pictures of you on my walls alone. I have another 500 or more that I've clipped from magazines and downloaded from the Internet.

I come for you each and every night.

I don't think you are tall, but in that picture, where you've got that cigarette hanging out of your mouth, your fingers pointing like pistols. You glare at the camera. I just want you to put that cigarette out in my mouth, to stomp it out on my tongue.

"Stick your tongue out!!"

"Yes, Mistress."

"Stick it out, I said!!!"

I push my tongue out further.

"Beg!!"

"Please Goddess Lynndie, put your cigarette out on my tongue."

You inhale hard and the tip of your smoke gets hotter.

I am on my knees. You stamp your cigarette on my extended tongue. My flesh sizzles. I come for you.

I am alone in my room.

I write to you, in care of the prison.

I wait in vain for your reply.

Perhaps they are not giving you my letters.

Lynndie, I lick your boots. I lick your ass. I lick you clean.

I want you to know.

I search GotWarPorn.com and YouTube.

I search and I yearn.

I know not heaven.

I grovel at your feet, Lynndie. I want to suck your toes. I adore you. I need you to know.

Sand

Ground stone—granite, gneiss;
    Tectonics and blown glass.
    Dragged and pulled,
    Strewn—
    Behind the vehicle, beneath the tires.
    Vandals in Carthage,
    Aridity,
    Conversion,
    Frederic drowns in the desert.
    Bodies chained to trucks—
    In Fallujah and Jasper, Texas.
    Dark dreams and high winds,
    Limbs loosed—
    Shattered, amputated, scattered;
    Everything scorned.
    Sand: loose particles of hard broken rock, a sedimentary material finer than
a granule and coarser than salt, small grains of worn or disintegrated rock.
    Moments of allotted time or duration.

John Milton

In the ditch I dream of civil power; I scrunch a book of poems from my knapsack—a treatise Sir Hill says.

We do not disagree about history.

The sky is strewn with ordnance like migrating birds.

Geese fly south.

The shooting stops and the screaming starts. Remnants of relatives await in the rubble.

I try to read.

I recall William Carlos Williams and the idea of dying for wont of poetry, or at least what is found there.

Wheelbarrows and cold, delicious plums.

I am uncommonly calm.

Closeby I hear coughing. Further away, wailing.

I read on: "It is not a matter of justice. Justice is in another world."

The next sentence I do not understand.

Then the sound of another bomb.

More screaming, cries.

I swear I can hear a dog bark.

Doubtful.

Someone, something sounds like a dog, somewhere.

I resume reading.

I imagine the Glorious Revolution!

In this ditch, my mind wanders.

Annie Ochs is my high school love. Annie Ochs is better looking than God. Annie Ochs feels like history.

I know that I am alone in a ditch.

I move my feet.

I hear more screaming.

I bear down on my book.

I should be doing something else, but I am not sure what else.

More screams, then I hear someone sneezing, over and over.

I start to laugh, uncontrollably.

Then another dog-like noise.

"Shut the fuck up," I hear.

I am unsure of the audience for the remark.

More noises I cannot decipher.

Annie Ochs had beautiful hands, long, thin fingers and shapely nails. Or has. I have not seen Annie Ochs in many years.

The bombing resumes. And, of course, the screams.

The humor of the sneezing.

Strikes me funny,

Though not.

The search for synonyms—screaming, wailing, crying; parched throats and parsed voices.

I had not considered dying here.

I bore into my book.

Obscure events intrigue me.

Runnymeade.

A funny wired, now at least; perhaps not then.

Nearby ditches fall silent.

Due to injuries perhaps; perhaps fatal.

I check myself for wounds. I have none. I am certain of that.

Of my next steps I am not so sure.

Still I read on.

This book is short. I do not have another book. Yet the Treatise's content is dense. I can occupy myself with it for quite some time. This little book means so much to me.

A Fucking Band-Aid

We take fire but fare well.

We have protection.

Thick walls serve us.

Desert winds obscure sight.

We light cigarettes.

Everything is the color of dirt.

It all changes.

Kelso screams.

He stops and he starts again.

I need a band-aid. I need a fucking band-aid.

I look at Kelso.

I think he is missing an arm.

The night before the shelling, Kelso had taken a Sharpie and written his name on every one of his limbs—forearm and upper arm calf and thigh, hand and foot—so that we could identify his body parts in case they were severed.

Kandahar

Corpses slow like cilia. Birds transmogrify, amber ale, polar opposites desalinate. Power plants below sea level. Mineral reserves. Her one long fingernail. I choose not to debate transubstantiation. Sloe gin fizz. The reporter's questions turn harsh. Slices of cheese. Burned to a crisp. I fail to see particulate matter. Reversing the follicles of the dead across the drawstring bridge. Surgical scrubs at the ready. The U.S. Army website. We never hear the phone ring.

Pallor re-established. Punk trees. Ever-ready. Explosive devices. Broke-down car. Shattered dawn. Shattered buildings. Cigarettes smoked.

Our hair is long, not golden. You drink my drink. I buy another. The world goes on, just not for us.

Closing Rites

Et cum spiritu tuo

Tonga

As he did most every night, Carol's husband came home from the bars in a drunken rage. I'd watched all the movies about Medgar Evers and Byron de la Beckwith. I'd learned driveway stalking technique. Carol had locked her husband out. He was pounding on the door. He started to kick it in. I heard her screaming. The kids had woken up. He was too drunk to see me. I admit: I shot him in the back. Most of his midsection splattered against the front door. I didn't mean to make it hard for her to clean up.

**

I held her hand at the funeral. We had been getting together a couple of times a week. No one knew. At least we didn't think so. I was just a friend of the family. The rumors exploded. Two or three women came forward. Mark—that was the late husband's name—had fucked them, abused them, beat them. It felt like a Dixie Chicks song. The cops said the investigation would remain open, then that they had suspects, then that the case was cold.

**

All this happened in Gulf Shores, Alabama—the lives, the pregnancies, the killing. Mark was a local boy, a redneck. I'd moved to Gulf Shores for a job—night manager at a Holiday Inn.

Immediately after Mark's death Carol was despondent.

"I'm moving back to Tonga."

Why?" I asked.

"I have family there. They'll help me raise the kids."

Her kids are funny looking—Pacific-Island-looking rednecks.

"You have me."

"Who are you?"

I walked out while she cried.

**

Tonga is an archipelago consisting of 171 islands, 48 of them inhabited.

I tried to plug her parents' address into my GPS, but I didn't haven any luck.

Carol has very large feet with widespread, splayed toes. She is always barefoot. I often stare at her feet. Her feet turn me on.

Mark and Carol used to drink White Zinfandel and listen to Slayer and Metallica and Guns and Roses. I've always liked "Sweet Child of Mine," but the rest of it is shit.

To console her, I began to bring over bottles of Sauvignon Blanc and Pinot Grigio.

I am from Los Angeles.

I played soccer with her kids, ages eight and eleven.

She started to like dry wines.

We slow danced to "In a Silent Way," and to Tom Waits songs when she was especially melancholy. She cried in my arms.

I made love with her slowly. I worshipped her feet.

We never woke the children.

**

I got a promotion. General Manager in Charlotte, North Carolina.

I asked her to move north with me. She did.

My star rose in the company. I got another promotion.

We began collecting champagne—Gosset, Dampierre, an occasional bottle of Krug.

We had friends over.

The kids became more graceful, more attractive.

My professional friends told me we were an "exotic couple."

We got married in a grand affair.

The kids, teenagers now, almost out of the house, lamented that we were becoming too affectionate. But they liked me. We listened to Thelonoious Monk, Portishead. We slept late on weekends, Carol gaining weight, me kissing her stomach, reveling in the odd beauty of her feet, adoring her bigger breast, licking her high and low, making love often, more often, all the time…. Charlotte Gainsbourg playing on the iPod.

**

Ten years in, I wanted to tell Carol my secret: that I had murdered Mark, that I had done it for her, to protect her, that I'd done it for the life we had now.

I made a nice dinner, broke out a bottle of Krug.

"What's the special occasion?" she asked.

"You," I said.

We got buzzed, not drunk. I was ready to speak. Instead, she began to talk.

"You know how much I love you," she said. "So I feel I can say this, get it out there…"

I took her hand, my stomach tight.

"I miss Mark sometimes…," she stammered. "I mean, I don't miss being with him…you know that….just…well, you know, we made kids together…and…"

Her voice stopped like a dropped cell phone call.

She wasn't crying.

Dishes still on the table, I took her hand and led her upstairs to bed.

I didn't say a word.

Little Joy

We drove west on Sunset into Echo Park.

Against our will, we stopped at Little Joy for a PBR.

"Should we call it a night?"

"I'm up for one more."

"One sounds good."

We'd had dinner in Little Tokyo, talking rapidly, excitedly for hours, drinking hot sake.

For our nightcap, we parked on the side street, up from El Compadre.

A tricycle was padlocked to the street sign on the corner. We recalled men in space suits, spray painting light posts outside the Frolic Room, but that was years ago.

The place was packed. The pool players could not pull back their cue sticks, the crowd was so tight.

Johanna is five foot four; I'm just over six feet. She led the way, smiling and saying excuse me, pushing through to the haphazard bar. I followed as best I could, unable to sneak deftly through the small spaces between people.

She got to the bar first. Johanna laughed as I finally snuck past a girl in a bunny hat. We drank a PBR, then another. We spoke loud to one another because we had to.

"Everything's different," I said.

"I liked it better when the walls had holes and the furniture was broken," she said.

"Me, too."

We tried to talk some more, but it got louder and beers began to spill. I got some bar napkins to dry her shoulder.

"If we leave now Empress Liquor will still be open," she said.

The Catholic Mass begins with a blessing: "Dominus Vobiscum."

I am partial to the Holy Spirit.

Outside on Sunset Boulevard, there were a few smokers. The rest of the crowd was still inside, crushing the bar for last call.

We smiled at our wisdom. We locked arms and walked away. As we turned up Quinteros towards our car, a dead cat lay sprawled on the sidewalk.

Johanna saw it first and screamed.

"Oh shit," I said.

"Is it dead?"

"Yeah, looks pretty bad."

"What should we do?"

"Let me try calling the city."

I called 411 on my phone and tried to reach animal control. The recorded message said I could hit "one" if it was an emergency. I couldn't imagine they would think so.

"They're closed," I said.

"I feel bad leaving it here."

"I don't know what else to do."

"Shit," she said. "Fuck."

I took her arm and we walked to the car.

At the liquor store we ditched our plans to buy champagne.

"What should we get?"

"Our other usual?"

She snagged a bottle of Pinot Grigio and we went to the counter to pay. We bought the wine and two packs of cigarettes and the clerk called me "boss" five times, as always, and we paid for our things and went up the hill to her apartment.

We drank until 3 AM, maybe four.

We tried as hard as we could not to talk about the cat, but the image of the dead animal persisted, would not subside.

When the wine was gone, Johanna poured us tequila. The tequila was left over from a party she'd had some weeks ago. We never drink hard stuff.

An hour or so later the sun rose pink and gray in the East LA sky. Johanna fell asleep on the couch.

I got up gently, trying not to wake her, kissed her forehead, and slipped out the door, pulling it shut and locked behind me.

As the sun continued rising, I drove back to the corner of Sunset and Quinteros. The dead cat was still there. I used some newspapers and an empty box I had in my car to scoop the cat up. I closed the flaps of the box and put the cat and its casket in my trunk, driving off to give it a proper burial. Using a lug wrench and a tire jack, I interred the cat just off the jogging path at the Silver Lake reservoir. I said a little prayer.

Johanna would be pleased with what I had done.

We had spoken our doxology: "...in saecula saeculorum."

After the funeral, I drove the few blocks home in the rising dawn. I pulled into my driveway. My satellite radio played The Stone Roses' "I Wanna Be Adored." I turned the volume up. I remembered I had not left a note for Johanna. Still sitting at the wheel, listening to John Squire's guitar, I sent her a text: "I'm home. I'm safe." I thought about the meaning of those words.I turned the car off and tried to do the same with my brain.

It was full morning. On my front porch, I lit a cigarette. My elderly neighbor was already awake and listening to the news. He is hard of hearing and from Slovenia. The program was blasting. I blew smoke at the sun to the strange sounds of the South Slavic tongue.

Epilogue

Ite in pace

Epilogue ("The Holy Ones")

Obstreperous asphalt,

argumentative light –

particle and wave;

Hand-in-hand—drunk, limping and triumphant,

We sway down the squalid street.

About the Author

Larry Fondation is the author of two novels *Angry Nights* and *Fish, Soap and Bonds*, and three short story collections *Common Criminals, Unintended Consequences* and *Martyrs and Holymen*.

His three most recent books feature collaborations with London-based artist Kate Ruth.

Fondation has lived in LA since the 1980s, and has worked for nearly 20 years as an organizer in South Los Angeles, Compton and East LA.

His first three books are being published in France by Fayard. The first, *Angry Nights* (FC2 National Fiction Competition Winner, 1994), translated as *Sur Les Nerfs* ("On the Edge"), appeared in French in January 2012. It was nominated for the 2013 Prix SNCF du Polar. The second, *Criminels Ordinaires* (Fayard), was published in February 2013.

Fondation is a recipient of a Christopher Isherwood Fellowship in Fiction Writing. He can be contacted at lfondation@aol.com.

www.ingramcontent.com/pod-product-compliance
Lightning Source LLC
Chambersburg PA
CBHW050819180626
46814CB00004B/1357